Dear Parent:
Your child's love of reading starts here!

Every child learns to read in a different way and at his or her own speed. Some go back and forth between reading levels and read favorite books again and again. Others read through each level in order. You can help your young reader improve and become more confident by encouraging his or her own interests and abilities. From books your child reads with you to the first books he or she reads alone, there are I Can Read Books for every stage of reading:

SHARED READING
Basic language, word repetition, and whimsical illustrations, ideal for sharing with your emergent reader

BEGINNING READING
Short sentences, familiar words, and simple concepts for children eager to read on their own

READING WITH HELP
Engaging stories, longer sentences, and language play for developing readers

READING ALONE
Complex plots, challenging vocabulary, and high-interest topics for the independent reader

ADVANCED READING
Short paragraphs, chapters, and exciting themes for the perfect bridge to chapter books

I Can Read Books have introduced children to the joy of reading since 1957. Featuring award-winning authors and illustrators and a fabulous cast of beloved characters, I Can Read Books set the standard for beginning readers.

A lifetime of discovery begins with the magical words "I Can Read!"

Visit www.icanread.com for information
on enriching your child's reading experience.

An Imprint of Sterling Publishing
387 Park Avenue South
New York, NY 10016

SANDY CREEK and the distinctive Sandy Creek logo
are registered trademarks of Barnes & Noble, Inc.

Everything Goes: Henry in a Jam
Text © 2012, 2013 by Brian Biggs
Illustrations © 2012, 2013 by Brian Biggs

This 2013 edition published by Sandy Creek by
arrangement with HarperCollins Publishers.

HarperCollins Publishers® and I Can Read Books® are registered trademarks.

ISBN 978-1-4351-5057-7

Manufactured in Dong Guan City, China
Lot #:
13 14 15 16 17 SCP 5 4 3 2 1
08/13

everything GOES

HENRY IN A JAM

Based on the Everything Goes books
by **BRIAN BIGGS**

Illustrations in the style of Brian Biggs
by **SIMON ABBOTT**

Text by **B.B. BOURNE**

Sandy Creek

Beep! Beep!

Henry is in the car.

He is going to a party.

The car goes up a hill.

The car goes down a hill.

The car stops.

Oh, no!

A tree is in the road.

All the cars stop.

Trucks stop.

Honk, honk, honk!

A big bus stops.

Henry waves.

10

The people wave back.

"Woof, woof, woof."

Henry sees a dog.

The dog wags his tail.

The dog does not want to stop.

The dog wants to see.

Who will move the tree?
Henry wants to see, too.

Dad gets out of the car.

Mom and Henry get out, too.

Henry still cannot see.

"Up here," says Dad.

"You can see better up here."

Now Henry can see.

Henry sees police cars.

He sees a fire engine.

He sees an ambulance.

"Is anybody hurt?" asks the driver

"No," says the policeman.

"That is good," says the driver.

"Great spot," the fireman says
to Henry.
"Better put this hat on!"

Henry sees a big truck.

Henry sees a backhoe.

"Over here!" says a policeman.

The big truck backs up.

The backhoe backs up, too.

"Ready, set, go!" Henry says.

The backhoe lifts.

The big truck pulls.

The tree stays.

"Oh, boy," says the man.

"Look!" says Henry.

"Here comes a crane!"

The hook goes down.

It hooks the tree.

Will the tree move?

Yes! The tree goes up.

The tree comes down.

The tree is off the road.

"Nice work,"
says the policeman.
Now the cars can go.

The trucks can go.

The bus can go.

The dog can go.

Henry can go, too.

"Happy birthday!" says Henry.